Selene 1

Selene Moon Goddess

Chapter 1
A Time of Happiness and Peace

Along the central part of Florida, to the northern gulf region of Texas, in the year of 1526 lives a peaceful tribe of simple people called the Ritke. The surrounding environment holds everything the Ritke need for shelter, food, water, shade and warmth. Simple meaning the Ritke live by what the earth provides for them. The Ritke live a life of wealth and abundance as this existence is the way there ancestors have lived for many generations from past to the present time. The Ritke have no need of riches or envy for they have never known of such things that corrupt other parts of the world. Or for that matter, that there is anything outside their part of the world. The Ritke hold value in family, friends, peace and the wealth in knowing that their part of the world provides all that they need to sustain their way of life.

Peaceful is the part of the world the Ritke share with their neighbors the Soto tribe also a peaceful people. The Ritke and the Soto live in harmony and trade back and forth when the need arises. Furthermore both tribes celebrate the new moon and give thanks to their God for the peace and the abundant, simple life they all enjoy. God provides the clothes made of the furs furnished by hunting the animals provided by their God, which gives them meat for nourishment. Plants, roots, and herbs, come from the ground in and around the village. A nearby plentiful river provides fresh water, fish as well as a place for the women to clean cooking pots and keep skins clean to wear.

The Shelters the Ritke dwell in are simple as well. These are made from waterproof leaves, broad and strong. The leaves are tied and woven into and around large strong young trees, stripped of branches. The larger animal skins drape across the entrance to the Shelters to provide warmth and protection from the rain for the Ritke. Some of the shelters are modest only made of one large room, for a couple. However, some are larger shelters with several rooms that are made to house large families.

There are individual tribe members who live together to help each other. The individuals have had loved ones pass on or have been taken during hunting accidents as well as misfortunes of everyday life in the landscape.

Although the tribe healers Jalen and his mate Asa tried to save all who have passed for whatever reason it was there time to go to be with their God. Jalen and Asa have lived in the village for thirty four years and all the tribe comes to them for their knowledge and natural medicine as well as their advice for illness. Jalen is considered quite young for a healer however he has great knowledge passed down to him from his father and grandfather. Jalen is tall and in strong health for a man of thirty four years and therefore his mate and his people depend on him very much. His long black hair is braided and his eyes are soft and kind a deep dark brown.

However, Jalen tends to most of the tribes needs as his mate Asa is with their second child to be born. Asa is small and petite she too has long black hair and her eyes say strength as they are a golden brown. This will be a special birth for a woman in her tribe her age. Asa was much younger ten years ago when she gave birth to their son Achiram, who is now ten and he wishes to be a healer and the best hunter the Ritke have ever had in the village. Jalen and Asa live on the outskirts of the village close to the river. The river provides fish, roots, moss, and water for much of the medicine needed for the Ritke and the Soto tribes.

The healers from the neighboring village, Jason and Rochelle have come to visit and stay until the birth of the second child. Both Jason and Rochelle are much older that Jalen and Asa so it is a comfort for Asa for them to visit and be near her now. Jason like Jalen has had healing in his family background for many, many years. As far back as the tribe has been in existence. Rochelle has always helped the sick and needy when and where ever she was needed. Rochelle just the past year gave birth to a beautiful tiny girl. Therefore Rochelle has her hands full with raising Amica now who is about one year old.

The tribes' people and the two villages have need of healers because even though there land is beautiful it holds great dangers. The rich botanical landscape is home to over 2,800 different species of plant life both friendly and poisonous. Therefore the tribes' children often mistake poisonous berries for the edible kind. In addition to the unfriendly plant life in the landscape there is also the threat of dangerous animal life.

Many accidents have occurred from dangerous encounters with poisonous insects' such as the Brown Recluse, although this species of spider is small its bite can make one extremely ill or if the individual has a weak immune system it can be deadly. Many other threats in the surrounding landscape include the black bear, wild boar and the panther. Any of these animals can become a threat quickly if intimidated or threatened or if they have young to protect. There have been incidents that villagers' have come to close and been attacked by these creatures who wandered to close to the village.

The plentiful river which gives water and fish to the villagers' also hold danger, with the threat of poisonous water snakes such as the Copper head, Cottonmouth, the Coral snake and even the Diamondback rattlesnake all come to the river for water, furthermore there is the ever present Alligator. Alligator's are very territorial and will defend their part of the river and attack humans to survive. Jalen and Asa have seen the results from encounters from each one of these dangerous threats and have had to treat the villagers when they are needed. Not all of the encounters results outcomes have been pleasant some villagers have lost their lives and loved ones to the animals and the landscape. With all of the knowledge in healing the both retain there is still some loss and suffering.

The balance of harmful wildlife and friendly wildlife is apparent in and around the village therefore Jalen and Asa use all the resources available to them to help the villagers stay well and comfortable when they are called upon.

For now the village is at peace and busy with preparation for the moon celebration. When the moon is full and most visible in the sky all the tribe members gather to celebrate and give thanks to their God for all they have and their families. The celebration entails each tribe member to dress in the finest furs. Jewelry made of shells and claws of the creatures used for food and garment. Each family and individual of the tribes brings the finest meats, fruits and roots for the great meal of abundance they have been blessed with.

This celebration of abundance is especially meaningful as Asa is very close to the birth of her second born child arriving. However with only two days until the celebration there is no time to delay there is much to do. There are ingredients to be gathered, fruits to be harvested as well as the meats to be hunted for the feast of abundance. Asa and Jalen choose to hunt a wild deer and prepare it at the celebration; therefore Jalen has to set off into the landscape to find just the perfect size to feed an entire tribe. As he begins his hunting day he debates to himself the fact that he will need a large male or Buck deer to provide enough meat. However if he should stumble upon more than one this day he will be truly blessed and there will be more than enough for all to enjoy. As he walks along further into the landscape he says his usual pre hunt prayer for luck, safety as well as forgiveness' for taking a living life. Jalen asks for forgiveness that he must take the life of a living creature even though it is a necessity it is the way of the Ritke.

Along his path he finds luck and spots a heavy track of a deer, this one is quite large as the impression is deep in the earth. Therefore he follows the tracks to see where it will lead him. With luck and soft steps he spots the large Buck grazing by a large tree unsuspecting and at ease the deer goes about his business. Jalen drew back the Long Bow and let loose his arrow. The arrow flies straight and true threw the heart of the large Buck and instantly the massive creature falls where it was grazing.

With the hunting trip being a success now he has to prepare the kill for transport back to the village. Jalen unsheathes his knife made of the wooden handle and blade of rock. First he retrieves his arrow from the kill then he removes the insides, this makes the kill lighter to carry the long trip back to the village. Still considerably heavy he bears the burden and begins his way back to the village hoping to arrive before the sun fades away in the sky. As Jalen begins his way back he thinks to himself this has truly been a blessed day, this Buck will feed many at the feast. Jalen also wonders what his mate Asa is busy with and he hopes that she is not overdoing her chores and preparations so close to the birth of their child.

As Jalen thinks of Asa she is back at the village busy gathering fresh bananas, mangos as well as the herbs she will need to season the meat her mate has gone to fetch for the feast. Asa also has to go to the river to draw pots of fresh water. The water will be used for cooking, washing the gathered fruits and the washing of their bodies before the feast. Asa decides to draw extra water in case it is needed and she may not have time to return to the river often. Once she has finished drawing the water; then carrying it all back to her simple dwelling.

She greets her guests Jason and Rochelle who are also busy preparing and crafting new bowls for the feast. These are made of wood as well as turtle shells. Large bowls are needed to be filled with various food goods for the feast of abundance. Asa congratulates and thanks them for all their hard work and their craftsmanship. As they all finish the things they are working on they see Jalen approach the dwelling with the Fine Buck draped over his shoulders. Jason rushes to help Jalen to lift the Buck off his tired shoulders and skin the body then to cut off the head and ready the meat for cooking the next day.

When the meat is made ready it is hung inside in a cool place for the night and all the friends say their goodnights and give their thanks for the wonderful day. Then it is time to rest until tomorrow and another busy day ahead.

The very next day bring the beautiful warmth of the sunlight and the entire village is making ready for the feast, guest from the Soto village begin to arrive and in a clearing beside the village they fashion tables of log and branches covered with palm leaves. This will be where all the different foods will be placed for all to enjoy. Furthermore three large fire pits are piled with dried branches and pieces of wood for the cooking of the fish, deer, and wild boar for the feast. Once the fires burn down to coals the meat is hung from sharpened small trees that have been soaked in the river to cook the meats, as well as the other foods that require fire for preparing. All the villagers work well into the afternoon the day before the feast so the next day all is left is to celebrate, visit, dance and give thanks to their God for the blessings. The villagers begin to retreat back to their dwellings for the night of rest with their guests from the Soto village.

Jalen and Asa and their guests Jason and Rochelle head back toward the river to their dwelling Asa begins to feel an uncomfortable pressure she decided she had done too much this day and it is nothing to worry over. However as they all reach to entrance to the dwelling about to retreat inside, Asa's water breaks. Jalen and Rochelle help Asa inside and make her comfortable; after all she is in good hands with three healers around her what could be safer. Asa begins to have contractions, small and discomforting contractions far apart this continues throughout the night and on into the next day, the day of the feast. Asa is disappointed that she will not be able to attend the feast and that the birth will keep her guests and Jalen from attending the feast. At the same time Asa is overcome with the joy of the birth of this child coming into her life.

The feast and celebration can be heard from the river and the smell of the food wafts over the breeze in the air. However Asa does not have time to worry over the goings on in the village she is preoccupied with the faster contractions and the stabbing pains coming closer and much faster now than before. The time draws near for the child is coming. Rochelle speaks softly to Asa and Jalen holds her hand and coaches her to focus and push when needed. Even though Asa is exhausted she focuses on Jalen's strong sounding voice. The moon is full and shines bright as daylight Asa pushes one last time as with all her being depends upon it and the child emerges from inside her.

However, there is no sound no wonderful cry or sounds that babies make. Rochelle calls to Jalen to come quickly. Jalen goes to Asa's Feet and sees the child is a girl but the child has been born with a veil. Jalen quickly takes a small sharp knife in his hand and skillfully removes the veil. He holds the child upside down and gives a small spat on the tiny bottom of the child. The child begins to cry and move with air and life within its tiny body. A true blessing not only was the child born during the feast of abundance and thanks, this tiny child was born with a veil. The veil to the Ritke means a special child born with great gifts. Not only has their God blessed them the Moon has blessed them as well. Therefore it seems only right to give this child a special name which means moon goddess Jalen and Asa decide her name will be Selene. With their second child now arrived Asa can rest with yet another blessing from their God.

Chapter 2
Growing Up

To the Ritke all life is precious; however the life of Selene was especially precious because of the circumstances' surrounding her birth. The moon the veil and the fact that these children brought great blessings to their villages all believe Selene would do the same for them. Selene had many blessings from the tribe members everyone watched out for her and her wellbeing. Asa had extra help with her needs while Selene was in her infant stage, everyone especially the women of the village wanted to take turns sitting with and carrying Selene. Asa supposed that they all though Selene would bring them good fortune and they too would be blessed with special children.

It gave great joy to Asa that all loved and accepted her new born child and were all so helpful and grateful. As Selene grew from infant to toddler she required even greater attention. She was walking and begins to wander and become curious about everything around her. Therefore Asa was truly grateful for the extra eyes and hands the tribe provided caring for Selene. Whether or not it was coincidence or just a really healthy time period for the tribe, Jalen and Asa seem to be needed less after Selene had been born. Some thought it strange but others were thankful. Life was the same peaceful and calm in the village and Selene continued to grow. Selene became good friends with Jason and Rochelle's Daughter Amica, who was only about one year older than Selene. Amica Didn't see what all the fuss was about over Selene she only saw a best friend and someone about her age to hang out and play with. Amica's parents had no other children but Amica was not spoiled or treated differently. She was a simple honest young girl who had kind loving parents. Amica and Selene were inseparable. If Amica was not at the Soto village she was with Selene and the same went for Selene. The girls did everything together. There was no need to worry over them getting into any kind of trouble. As long as they stayed between the two villages they would be looked after. The Ritke and the Soto all looked after and cared for each other's young ones. After all the young people will be the future of the tribes' existence.

Selene and Amica had many things in common their parents were all healers in their tribes, their tribes were neighbors and friends. Amica and Selene both discovered their love of animals and they like to paint rocks and trees with different colored berry juice they made of smashing berries with rocks. Amica had real talent painting her trees and animals turned out realistic, Selene however did not take to the art as easily her pictures turn out sickish and plain. They both loved to sit at the river; the clear water reviled the pretty colored fish and the strange small creatures with tiny pinchers where their hands should be. However, to the girls thought these were amusing creatures to watch and play with.

The girls were also fascinated with the men and boys working with some large creatures they called the horse, Amica and Selene would sit upon a small hill and watch the men teach the older boys how to handle and to ride these creatures. It was amazing to watch and even more amazing to see that the men and boys could sit on the horses back and the creatures would carry a man around. Amica and Selene wished they could sit and ride these beautiful creatures, but this was considered too dangerous for a woman in the tribe. As the horse is a wild and powerful animal and can easily hurt even the men that work with them.

As Selene watched she decided in her mind that one day she would sit on the back of one of the most beautiful horses that either tribe had ever seen. Selene decided that of all the creatures she had encountered that she likes the horse the most. Horses seemed to be the most useful creatures of all. She watched the men along with her brother as they would gently pet and lead the horses around with a thin small rope. Therefore Selene decided she could do even better than that she would one day get a horse to do anything she wanted without using anything but her hands and her voice. If she only knew just how real that thought would one day be.

Amica on the other hand liked the smaller strange creatures; she had even made a pet of one peculiar creature. Selene thought the creature was strange it was small and had tiny ears and feet and a small tail, but its body was covered in spiny hard thorns no one really knew what to make of it or to call the creature as it was eating small insects in the ground. This small creature would eat any and all insects it could find and even the ones Amica would offer it. Amica calls it her sticky pig and carried it with her everywhere she went in a skin pouch that her father made her for the creature. Selene did admit the sticky pig was kind of cute in its own way. The little pig was so tiny it fit in the palm of their tiny little hands quietly.

On one occasion Selene and Amica sat and watched the goings on of the adults in and around the village. Amica asked Selene what she wanted to be when she reached her adult age. Selene though for a long while and said a healer of course. Amica decided that was her desire also. Then all of a sudden Selene explained not a healer of humans but of the animals. Amica argued with Selene that humans were much more important and needed healing more than animals as her father Jason had taught her. However Selene disagreed and had made up her mind to convince her father and mother to teach her all they could and knew about healing and helping all creatures in the landscape.

Childhood was full, fun and educational to the girls, it was even exhausting some nights the girls would fall fast asleep soon after the evening meal. All to rise again the next day out in the landscape discovering new exciting things. Both Amica and Selene had to get all of their childhood adventures and play time out of their systems before they reach the age of fourteen. The Ritke and Soto childhood ended when the child turned fourteen.

After the age of fourteen the child had to turn from childish things and learn a skill useful to the tribe and learn to live and provide for his or herself. Moreover the women learned to cook, harvest and hunt for survival.

It seemed that the childhood and play time grew shorter with each passing day Amica being one year older than Selene, was soon to put away the things of a child and learn the things a woman should know. Only three months left until Amica was to turn fourteen years of age. So each day the girls spent together was precious time they would never have again.

Together at the edge of the river they both sat with their backs to the rocks, Amica playing with her sticky pig while Selene a few feet away was gathering pretty shells not paying attention. Selene failed to see the Coral Snake behind Amica coming down the rocks to the river for its daily drink. Suddenly Amica let out a shrill scream filled with pain and anguish. When she moved to pick up Sticky to protect it from the snake the snake bit her on the hand. Amica dropped Sticky and curled up instantly in pain.

Selene seeing and realizing what has just happened, quickly found a large sharp rock and threw it at the snake killing it smashing its head. Although it was too late for her best friend, Selene realized by the time she went to get her Father Jalen and explain what had taken place her friend would be gone. However Selene ran as fast as her legs and strong young muscles would carry her. As Selene made it to the opening to her dwelling her mother Asa was about to leave Jalen was not home. Asa had not treated this kind of a snake bite before never the less she hurried as fast as she could to the young girl to do what she could. Asa had grabbed two vials of medicine from a shelf to help Amica. Unsure of whether they would work or not she had to try. Selene and Asa arrived back at the river quickly, however Asa could see that Amica had been bitten to high on the arm close to her neck, therefore the poison had quickly traveled to Amica's head and heart. Asa tried to get Amica to drink the one vile of medicine, it was no use she could not swallow Amica's body had already been seized by the Coral snakes toxic venom. Asa looked sadly back at Selene and said we are too late. Amica managed to point to her little pig Sticky and she looked lovingly at Selene as if to say take care of him and I love you my friend! Amica then closed her eyes and her spirit left her body.

Selene took Sticky and held him close as she sobbed over the loss of her precious best friend. If she had only been paying attention, if she had run faster, if she were skilled in the craft of healing she could have saved her best her only friend. Selene said to her mother "I HATE SNAKES in fact I HATE ALL ANIMALS". Even though she clung to Sticky now he was all she had of Amica and she would protect him forever!

Asa Carried the body of Amica back to her humble dwelling, now she and Jalen had to tell their best friends there only child was gone forever. How would she find the words? When Jalen returned he was shocked to see the body of the girl and to hear what had taken place. Jalen decided and had his son go and get his horse to take the body home to her parents. Achiram returned with a strong beautiful black horse. The horse had a long amazing mane and tail. The horse was gentle and kind therefore a travois was fashioned upon the horses back, around his middle and chest with strong strips of skins. The skins were soft to prevent rubbing and sores to form on the horse drawing the travois. Amica's lifeless body was carefully laid upon the travois and Jalen, Asa, Achiram and Selene began the journey to take the girl's body home.

A short journey to the Soto village seemed to take a life time as they all walked along side and behind the horse. They came to the edge of their own village the whole tribe was filled with sorrow for the loss of this young beautiful life. It seemed so senseless but all the tribe members knew in their hearts all things happen for reasons they do not understand and maybe never will. With the explanations given to all who did not know the group managed to get to the outskirts of the Ritke village. The group grew larger as more friends of Jason and Rochelle heard and felt the need to go to them at this time of loss. So with a group finally totaling eight they reached the Soto village.

The news of the loss traveled fast amongst the Soto's, Jason and Rochelle stood in front of their home and met the devastated stares of Jalen and Asa and the horse drew ever closer. Rochelle walked to the side of Asa and knelt down to the body of her daughter she wept quietly. Asa hugged her and explained the incident to her dear friend. Asa told her how truly sorry she was for the lost of Amica and that she had tried to help the girl. Rochelle was kind and replied "I am sure you did everything you could for her. It was Gods will He needed her beautiful paintings she created."

Jalen explained to Jason how he was in the village tending to a child who's arm had been cut on a rock while playing. "I am truly sorry I was not there maybe I could have saved her." Jalen held his friends hand and asked what was needed of him and his family. As did the rest of the Ritke that had come to offer comfort. They all took Amica's body inside to begin the cleansing and burial ceremony for the girl and her parents. The ceremony took two days to complete. There was a meal prepared for Jason and Rochelle to end the ceremony then Jalen Asa Achiram and Selene all began their Journey back to the Ritke village and home.

Selene began to feel better and less lost after several weeks had passed, although she still missed Amica it would take time to heal the loss and the guilt Selene felt. Selene told her mother she had no need for child things and wished to learn the craft of a healer. She no longer wanted to heal animals she wanted to heal and save people. Therefore Asa spoke to Jalen to see if he would allow her to put aside the last year of her childhood and become a woman with a skill.

Jalen would have to teach Selene the things that have been passed down from his father and grandfather. He considered this a lot of knowledge for such a young person to learn. However Jalen knew that Selene was gifted even though he did not know what kinds of gifts she truly had. Jalen felt they would surface soon enough. So he and Asa began to teach Selene the craft of healing. At thirteen Selene learned quickly and her parents could see that she would be a kind and gentle healer. Sticky would lay in Selene's lap or by her and sleep as she studied the plants, roots and what each one did to heal the different parts of the human body. Selene also learned that sometimes it required multiple concoctions of plants roots and herbs for some illnesses. She began to master and memorized each mixture and how it should be taken or giving.

Jalen and Asa only let Selene study the healing and the medicines until she reached the adult age of fourteen. Then she could venture out into the landscape and learn how to survive on her own. Each child at fourteen had to be taken outside the village, given a knife, a skin, and string and must survive for three days alone. This was the way of the Ritke no exceptions even for the women. After all if she is not strong enough to live alone three days then the future children she bears will also be weak and die.

Jalen and Achiram walked Selene a half days walk from the village, gave her the required items she needed and they turned to return to the village. With the instruction to still be there or meet them in three days time. Easy enough Selene already knew what plants and roots she could survive on. However she was also instructed to build a small snare and catch a rabbit. Selene had to produce a rabbit foot as proof she had succeeded. The snare was easy and she had the knife to process the rabbit however the fire to cook the rabbit could prove tricky.

She had seen her brother Achiram take two special stones and strike them together, as she thought to herself she should have paid more attention. Never the less she began to grab stones and strike them together to see if they would make fire. After several different combinations and sizes she found two small flint rocks that worked well. Selene put these in the outside of Sticky's pouch with the twine and began to fashion a snare out of the twine and small low branches. The trick was to place the snare where the rabbit travels frequently for it to become ensnared. After the snare was in place she knew she had to hurry to gather wood for a fire, the fire even a small one would ward off the dangerous creatures in the area. Furthermore larger wood and branches would provide a small temporary shelter for her three day stay in the landscape.

While gathering the much needed branches and wood she heard a small rustling behind her. Selene quickly though of the day at the river this event haunted her memory she was sure there was an evil snake close by she looked around and found another huge rock ready to bash whatever emerged from the underbrush she held the rock high and readied herself. However much to her surprise out bounded a plump white rabbit for a moment the rabbit sat distant and watched Selene with big red eyes. Then as if to be friendly and greet her as her best friend the rabbit bounced up along to her feet. Rock ready to end this creature and claim her much needed prize Selene could not bring herself to take this small friendly life. Even though she had vowed she hated all animals when her friend had died. This was truly a strange little creature not to fear a human much less one with a rock poised to take its very life. Selene relaxed her hands and slowly lowered the Hugh rock. She knelt down and the rabbit moved even closer to her body.

Once Selene decided that she had a new friend she busied herself with the task at hand gathering more wood for the fire and fashioning a small makeshift shelter. When the shelter was done she took the knife and dug around for some edible roots and plants to tide her over until the snare provided a more suitable meal. The plump rabbit continued to stay close to Selene as a lifelong friend had just returned to her and missed her immensely. Therefore she allowed the rabbit stay and visit.

Next was the task of finding water before dark and building the fire for warmth and protection. Selene looked around and found a patch of extremely green plants and trees in one area; this meant that there must be a water source near the green foliage. Sure enough as Selene walked along she began to hear a trickle of a tiny stream a few hundred feet from where she had made her small shelter. Now the task was to derive a way to contain the fresh water and carry it back to the shelter.

Selene had seen her mother take a large leaf and roll the leaf tight at one end then tie the end with a vine and use this to drink from so she found the same kind of leaf and did the same as she had seen her mother do and it worked very well. The leaf was large enough to hold plenty of water for the night.

Selene reached her small make shift shelter, she then poured out a small amount of the water for the plump rabbit and Sticky. As she watched them drink she decided that the plump rabbit must have been someone's pet and that was why the rabbit was fearless of humans. Never the less she was growing tired after the full day walking then making her shelter so she gathered several handfuls of dry grass and hit the two stones together until the sparks caught to the grass and began to smoke. Once the grass burned well she added small twigs then larger sticks until Selene had a moderate size fire. She was secure in knowing the fire would light the area and keep away large animals while she rested for the night.

Selene lie down and fell asleep quickly, Sticky rooted around in the soft earth finding a snack as the insects drew closer to the fire. The plump rabbit lay close to Selene and watched Sticky for a while the rabbit also rested for the night. Sticky being a nocturnal creature foraged most of the night then returned to the safety of his small skin pouch close to Selene.

The sun began to peek around the small shelter Selene had slept in and when it hit her eyes she began to open them. Not fully awake she heard a wakeful cry the sound of an animal injured or in great pain. The sound came from the area where she had placed the snare. Selene quickly and carefully moved toward the sound sure enough the snare had caught its quarry. In the snare she found a medium size brown rabbit, hung by the neck. Selene was sad for the life the snare had taken at the same time she was proud that she had succeeded in her mission. Selene took out her knife and as she has seen her brother do countless times she began to skin and prepares the rabbit for cooking.

Once the rabbit was over the small fire cooking and the rabbit's foot tucked away in her pouch Selene sat and observed the landscape around her. For the most part it was full of thick foliage green and plush. Then she noticed something strange small creatures and birds sat all around her. The birds were not singing and the small furry animals just sat and watched to see what Selene would do next. Selene was amazed that these creatures were curious as to what she was and what she was doing and not running for their lives. Nothing such as this had ever happened to her before and she did not remember any stories of it ever happening to any other tribe member either.

Even in the distance she could see larger animals' deer and even fox were all around her. Selene became a bit nervous and even slightly scared questions began to run through her head. Why was this happening, what were they there for why had they come why were they drawn to this area? This was the strangest thing she had ever seen. Selene wondered what would happen if she moved or approached the animals. Still slightly unsure of the situation she took the knife in hand and slowly rose and moved toward the small cluster of creatures. None moved as she reached out with knife in hand to touch them in fact they moved even closer toward her. They all wanted to be as close to her as possible. She put away the knife and stood in amazement all the hatred she had been harboring for animals faded away. Love filled her heart as she felt love and affection all around her.

Selene spent the rest of the day being with, and playing with all the creatures gathered around her, the questions still ever present in her mind what is going on. On into the night the animals stayed close to her until she was exhausted and finally fell asleep.

Chapter 3
Discovering New Gifts

The next morning arrived with the sun peeking around the small shelter. The shelter had served its purpose as soon Selene's Father and Brother would arrive to escort her home. Selene lay still for a few moments but turned her head to see if she had been hallucinating the prior day. However she looked and they were gone. No animals anywhere not even the plump white rabbit could be seen. In fact the only thing moving around her was the small soft skin pouch that Sticky was moving around in.

The events of the last two days were a conundrum who would ever believe that she was a magnet for animals especially after the death of her best friend she vowed she hated all animals. That hatred faded the prior day. Before too long Selene saw her father Jalen and her Brother Achiram walking toward her, should she tell them about the animals or leave that part out? Selene decided she would tell her mother when she is safe at home; mother would know what was wrong with her.

Selene walked along with Jalen and Achiram she showed them the rabbit's foot and told them the details of the fire and the shelter. As well as the water and how she had imitated her mother's example. Furthermore how well it had worked. All the way home the three talked amongst themselves and discussed how well Selene had done on her adult quest. However she kept the strange circumstances' about the animal encounters to herself; as she did not want her whole family to think she was insane. It took the better part of the morning to reach her home back by the river. Once safe and sound inside her dwelling she was tired however she desperately needed to speak to her mother about the events of the prior day.

"Mother, may I talk with you for a while something has happened that I don't understand" Selene asked her mother. Asa replied "of course darling child let us walk down to the river and talk along the way." Asa and Selene had walked half way to the river before Selene began to tell her mother that there was something wrong with her. Selene began the story about the plump white rabbit with the red eyes, also even further to explain that every animal in the area deer, fox, porcupine, rabbits, even creatures she had never seen before stranger than Sticky. Even stranger is the fact that the next morning they were all gone: "Mother, what is wrong with me was I seeing, or even imagining things."

Asa began to smile as she reached for Selene's hand, "still your mind child ease yourself and let me explain the circumstances' of your birth". Asa explained to Selene that when she was born it was the Celebration of Abundance under a full moon. As well as the fact that Selene was born with a Veil upon her face, the veil meant that she would be special and have special gifts and abilities. The Ritke tribe had only had a total of eight individuals born with a veiled face since the tribe has been in existence. Until now however no one knew if or when your gifts would surface. In some special individuals it takes many years for gifts to be discovered. Furthermore few born with a veil never discover their gifts. Selene felt much more at ease and comforted. However Asa also said she alone would have to discover what the gifts meant and how to use them! After their discussion they walked back to the shelter and began to prepare the evening meal.

Asa was joy filled as she and Selene told Jalen and Achiram the wonderful news of the gift of Selene's ability to draw creatures to her. Even though Selene explained she'd not known how it had happened they just appeared from the landscape and stayed a long while.

Jalen encouraged Selene that she should spend more time out in the landscape and learn all she could about this wonderful gift given by the Moon God. Jalen explained that this gift could be of great benefit to the Ritke as well as their friends the Soto tribe. Therefore soon Selene settled in for a long nights rest to do exactly what her father suggested. Selene would spend the day on the other side of the river tomorrow alone, and see what if any results the day might bring about!

Selene hardly slept as she was filled with joy from the tail her mother had told about her birth and the circumstances' that surrounded her very existence. In fact Selene was up as early as her mother. Asa was surprised to see Selene up so bright and early, however she smiled at her and began to gather bread and fruits and a gourd full of milk for Selene to take with her on her day outing past the river. Selene set out soon after the meal was stuffed into the skin bag her mother gave her. So with Sticky on one hip and the meal bag on the other she was on her way to the landscape past the river.

Selene found a spot that was plush and green with soft grass surrounding her, and a few short steps away was a good place for Sticky to root around for insects and roots if he so wanted to. Selene took out a medium size banana and began to peel it back; as she did she heard the sounds of leaves rustlings close to her. Selene sat very still and waited, she watched as two deer came closer and closer, two more emerged from the landscape. A few moments later rabbits appeared so many she lost count. Then foxes, porcupine and all matter of small furry creatures' surrounded her. Selene knew not to fear the animals however this time she was faced with the task of discovering why animals are drawn to her. Thinking to herself Selene debated how to communicate with them. She closed her eyes and sat very still, cleared her mind and concentrated on a Porcupine that stood in front of her. Several minutes had passed and she was just about to open her eyes when she felt a nose twitching cool to the touch in her hand. Thoughts began to fill her head, hello will you be a friend to me no one likes me because I look strange. Selene was sadden she opened her eyes and spoke to the little porcupine and said yes of course I will I am strange too. So strange in fact I do not even understand myself.

Selene felt laughter from the touch of the creature and joy that it understood her words and thoughts. Selene decided to see if she could tell the little porcupine to come and lay beside her so it could be her first friend. She touched the nose and the porcupine walk to her side and lie down closed its eyes and relaxed. Selene felt out of place incomplete since Amica was taken from her. Only now did Selene begin to understand her place in this world. After the little porcupine lay beside her Selene decided to see if the other animals would come to her as well, she did the same as before closed her eyes and concentrated on a deer not too far away, Selene thought the words in her mind "Why have you come to me?" Again she felt the nose of a creature nuzzle her softly. "I have come with my mate to receive your blessing for our fawn soon to arrive." In front of her stood a large proud Buck Deer and close to him was a rather round female deer. Selene could tell the doe was indeed carrying a fawn. Therefore Selene closed her eyes and touched the Bucks Nose once more. "I would gladly grant a blessing if I had the power to do so; however I am a simple girl not a god with powers to guarantee healthy life".

Immediately Selene's mind flooded with the words "Yes you do have the power we have all watched you as you have grown You Are The One Moon Goddess Madam Selene". Selene removed her hand from the nose of the Buck in shock Goddess? How is that possible? Selene could tell the Buck was old and wise. However Asa never said anything about a Goddess?

Selene again closed her eyes and thought the words in her Mind. "How do you know this who told you?" The Buck Stood up straight and looked to the heavens then lowered his nose back to Selene's hand. "The Sun told us one would be born under the full moon that would bless and help us. To watch for her and do all we can to protect her". Therefore we have watched you since your birth until you became aware of this great gift. Selene sat back and was truly amazed to learn of all this. To learn she was a Goddess what did this mean what were her responsibilities, could she in fact ensure blessings and health to the unborn fawn.

Selene thought a great deal about this and again she closed her eyes as she looked at the doe. Please come to me she thought in her mind. The doe responded and came close to Selene. Selene got up and knelt on one knee to place her hands around the belly of the doe. Once her hands were in place Selene softly though these words. "I bless this birth of this fawn, may it be born healthy and strong and grow too many long years of age in our landscape." The doe stood very still as her tummy tingled while Selene's fingers felt like someone had plunged her hands in ice cold water for a moment then the feeling was gone. The doe looked at Selene lowered her nose to touch her hand the words Thank you popped into Selene's Mind. The great Buck in turn did the same thing to say thank you for the blessing received.

Selene spent the entire day mentally speaking with each animal discovering each one of their needs. Selene dealt with each creature large and small. Some of the issues that the animals brought forth Selene did not know how to deal with however she made sure that the animals knew they would find the answers together and as soon as possible.

When the day was nearing its end Selene was ecstatic she could not wait to get home and share with her family her new found gifts and the information the Buck had shared with her about who she truly was. Furthermore her true purpose in this life. The statement Selene had made to her young friend Amica was inevitably true she truly was a healer of animals both large and tiny. However Selene still had much to learn about healing animals, as well as dealing with their individual needs and concerns.

Once back at her simple dwelling she shared the events of the day and the information the great Buck had shared with her about who and what she truly was. A Moon Goddess however you look at the title being a Goddess of any kind is a huge responsibility especially for one so young at fourteen years of age. Much less not fully understanding the full extent of her gifts and how powerful they truly are. Both Jalen and Asa agreed the more time Selene spent with the creatures out in the landscape the greater her knowledge and her power would grow. Therefore the very next day she would venture out again into the landscape and spend time with her destiny.

Chapter 4
Magnificent Bodacious the Horse Lord

As planned the very next day Selene was up even before the Sun had time to rise in the sky. She had planned to venture out past the river where it begins to flow into the sea. Therefore Selene set out on her way, just outside the porcupine lay still sleeping awaiting Selene and to see what the two of them would be doing this day. Selene knelt down and touched the creature on the nose and mentally explained the plan to him. The porcupine rose slowly and waddled alongside her for the long walk ahead.

As the two of them walked Selene remembered her mother stating that close to the great sea lived an older woman alone. The woman had never found a mate and she was gentle and kind however she had mentioned that it was lonely and wished she had a companion. Selene thought this was the perfect match for her strange little friend the porcupine. Furthermore she would venture by the woman's home on the way to the great sea and see if she could help the porcupine find a real loving place of his own.

The two of them continued to walk slowly as they walked Selene softly spoke to the little creature of her plans to help him find his place and this would be the solution to his loneliness as well as the old woman. Slowly an uneasy feeling began to fill Selene's mind. Her body began to shake with fear her thoughts were filled with the words blood, kill, hungry, and food. Selene stopped stood very still and knelt beside the porcupine however before she could touch the nose of the porcupine she heard the most awful cry she had ever heard in her life in fact she had never heard this sound before in her life.

What should she do where should she go, what was the source of the terrible sound. Again she heard the awful sound it ripped through her body and made her shiver with fear. Slowly and stealthily a large shinny black four footed creature walked out into the open. Selene could see that it had long great white teeth as well as the size of its body was massive and powerful. Selene closed her eyes and tried to communicate with the creature, however she kept receiving the same dangerous words in her head and the feeling of fear filled her body. Selene could hear and feel the Panther breath and almost smell and taste the blood the great cat lusted for in her mouth.

Selene though quickly what should I do, suddenly she heard a sound familiar but it was distant then the sound grew louder she thought to herself now what could that be. Louder the sound grew in her ears, as the Great cat paced back and forth in front of her. Just as Selene was sure the Panther was going to leap and attack a large mass slammed into her body throwing her back and out of the great cats reach. Selene landed on her back and once she regained her thoughts she saw what had knocked her away from danger. Before her eyes between her and the Panther stood the biggest most beautiful spotted horse she had ever seen. This horse was unlike any the Ritke had in the village. Its muscles rippled with tension the horse reared and struck out at the great cat. Selene could barely see the cat for the long flowing white mane and tail the horse grew from its body. Again and again the Horse struck out at the great cat.

The cat grew more and more aggravated that it was being cheated out of its meal. Therefore it tried repeatedly to find a way around the massive horse's sharp hooves. However it was useless the horse was unrelenting everything the great cat tried the horse was too fast and would not move from between him and the girl he wanted. The panther moved to the right and tried to slip past the horse but the horses right hoof struck the cat's eye blood began to flow from its face and pain filled the cats head. The fight between the two wild beasts seemed to go on for a lifetime even though it was only several moments once the great cat realized that the meal was not worth him being injured further or even killed by the stallion he slowly backed away from the situation and slithered back into the landscape.

Selene finally drew a full breath and began to relax her body and mind, she then looked and the porcupine that had sought refuge behind her. The porcupine was untouched though thoroughly shaken. Selene's attention turned back to the horse her thoughts of how magnificent the creature was. How the horse had saved her and the porcupine, but why had he and how did he know their lives were in danger. Why couldn't she have communicated with the Panther and told him they were of no threat to him. Selene supposed that the great cats hunger was stronger than his reasoning.

Once the situation was calm and all had returned to normal the horse had calmed down though still tossing his head he looked into Selene's eyes. Selene mentally said thank you to the Horse and told him to come to her and she would bless him. However the horse just stood his ground and shook his head as if to say no. Selene stood in disbelief that the horse did not succumb to her command. Again politely she mentally asked the horse to come to her to receive her blessing. Once again the horse stood his ground and shook his long beautiful mane in a no gesture. This began to anger Selene she mentally spouted the words 'I AM THE MOON GODDESS SELENE AND YOU ARE BOUND TO DO AS I ASK OF YOU". The horse looked at her and snorted at her thoughts. He was not impressed furthermore he had no master. The horse walked toward Selene and put his nose in her hand. Selene heard the horse's words clearly in her head. "I need not a blessing of a Human; I am Bodacious, horse lord of this landscape". "It is you who should be grateful to me and receive my blessing for saving you and your friend". Furthermore she heard the words humans come into my heard and force my kind to serve you and break their spirits. I only saved you because you travel with the spiny rat.

I do accept your thanks. The horse turned to leave and Selene said Stop! Selene looked into the horses' eyes then she closed her eyes and explained to the horse that she recently discovered the gift granted to her from God. That she was destined to help all creatures once she understood their needs and their pain. Selene said she could help him even though he was the lord of the horses. "How can you help you cannot give back the Spirits of my loved ones you have broken to serve you". Selene replied "yes I think I can. Come with me and I will do my best to give back what has been taken from you and your kind". First we must go to a small home where and older woman lives, you will see some of what I can do for animals.

Soon they all arrived at the home of the lonely old woman, Selene sat down with the woman and told her how lost and lonely the little porcupine was and how no one loved him because he was strange and odd looking, the old woman was delighted that Selene had brought her a lifelong friend to pass the time of day with. The little Porcupine bounced with joy and was very happy to have another friend and a place to call his! Selene said her goodbyes and told them to send word if they needed anything and that she would visit them often.

Selene and Bodacious journeyed back to the Ritke village as she had promised to rectify the situation and the anger the horse Lord harbored for humans. While walking Selene tried to decide how and what she could do or even if she was capable of a solution to the task that faced her now this was a huge responsibility. First she had to convince her kind to release the horses in the village, then the even bigger chore of restoring the spirit of any horse that had been broken or taken away by force.

At the Ritke village everyone stared and watched as Selene walked through the village with this amazing proud creature at her side. The horse was not afraid in fact if anyone got to close to him he snorted and they would back off. Selene asked all the horsemen to gather around as she explained the Horse Lords situation, his love, and concern for the horses. As Selene as the interrupter the men and the Horse Lord finally came to an agreement. Selene must talk to each horse and determine if he or she wished to stay with their human captors or if they wished to be freed?

If they wished to stay they could furthermore their spirits would be restored, even though Selene hadn't figured out quite how she would do that yet. First she had to begin speaking with each horse and see if they wished to be free or to stay and work alongside his or her human. Surprisingly many of the horses had never known freedom and the wild life so they did choose to remain with the promise that they would never be mistreated or harshly spoken to. Then once each horse had decided Selene asked the ones whose spirit had been taken or lost to stand to one side and she would do her best to restore it. Selene though back to the deer fawn and how she had laid her hands on the doe and she felt magic flow through her fingers. This time she thought of the Horse Lord. Selene pictured him in her mind running as fast as he could with his head held high, the long flowing mane and tail rippled and flowed in the air as he ran. She felt as if she were atop him and the freedom and joy she felt to be young, strong and unstoppable filled her entire body. Selene reached out to touch and older mare and the elated feeling surged from her hands to the mare's old tired body. The men around watching this event take place could not fathom what they saw! The old mare's color of pure silky reddish brown began to return to her coat. Her tired eyes opened widely, low hanging head rose high and proudly! The tired old muscles began to tone and her hooves grew strong and supple. The mare broke the grip of Selene's hands whirled and ran off a little way she jumped, kicked out and whinnied with delight.

The old mare then returned to the Horse Lord and Selene she gently put her nose in Selene's small hand and Selene heard the words thank you and bless you in her mind. Selene had done it she had restored the spirit the old mare has lost along her life as a human servant. Selene continued to restore the spirit of every horse that had been lost. This greatly pleased Bodacious and he was then truly grateful to the young Goddess and he deemed her worthy of his respect. The Horse Lord put his nose into the hand of Selene and she heard "You are truly worthy of my respect Thank You for all that you have done for my kind. We shall not forget this day. If you should ever have need of me just think of me, I shall come to you! I owe you a great deal for the work you have done here today"! The Horse Lord turned; his kind young and new born followed him to go back to their part of the landscape. Selene was both exhausted as well as pleased with what she had done. She hurried home to tell her family what had taken place this day once she had answered all the questions her family had she rested from the tiring day's events. Selene wondered what the next day would bring as she faded off to sleep. The following weeks proved productive and eventful. Selene discovered many things about the gift she had been blessed with she learned she could throw her thoughts without touch. She also discovered she had the ability to heal some animals of minor illness with a touch. Selene could even summon the gentle creatures of the landscape however; she could not summon or communicate with the predatory animals. Predators killing nature and instinct for survival made them unreasonable. Therefore, Selene continued her work with healing and dealing the animals and their needs.

Chapter 5
Felipe Lover of the Horse

In a few short months Selene and animals survived in harmony with the members of both the Ritke and Soto tribes. Although humans survived on mostly meat provided by hunting animals Selene convinced the tribes to hunt outside the landscape that surrounded both villages. Furthermore the hunters were to only take the lives of ill or older crippled animals. This compromise worked well. Moreover harmony and balance like never before had come to the Ritke and the Soto villages.

As Selene walked to a different part of the landscape to seek out more animals to help she noticed a lean young man watching the horses and the men working with them. As Selene approached him he looked at her then quickly turned away. Selene had seen and heard of this young man the story was he is from the Soto tribe. When the young man was just a small boy both his parents had been taken by a strange illness. The young man was brought to the Ritke by a friend of his parents. However the young man named Felipe was a shy and quiet sort of person.

Felipe had no friends to speak of and stayed to himself as he was always alone. As Selene came up to Felipe she spoke softly "hello you are Filipe are you not?" Felipe replied "yes I am um I'm afraid I do not know your name, though I have heard of the great things you have done." "My name is Selene, I am known as The Moon Goddess". "It is a blessing to meet you Selene". Felipe said to her. "Thank You" Selene replied! "Why do you sit all alone up here? Selene asked the young man. "I like to watch the horses I find them exquisite"! "They are fascinating creatures"! Felipe told Selene. "Horses are my favorite animal as well, I think they are amazing"! I have always dreamed of riding the most beautiful horse in the landscape however he is much too proud"! He is the Horse Lord Bodacious but I do not know what his name means". "You have met this Horse Lord"? Felipe Asked Selene. "Yes I have in fact I have helped him and his kind with a major problem that had existed for many years". Selene told Felipe the story as well as the outcome. That is fantastic I would love to see this amazing creature just to stand in his presence" Felipe said to Selene. "Well he is a friend of mine would you like to meet him" Selene asked Felipe. "Yes I would, could I" asked Felipe. Felipe's eyes lit up with joy and excitement as he bounced to his feet ready to go! Selene said very well then, come with me.

The two of them walked along softly talking among themselves asking each other things like what they liked to do games they liked to play. The two of them were vastly becoming friends as they laughed and got to know each other intently. It took several hours to reach the land where the horses dwelled. The horses preferred to be away in private away from the humans therefore Selene and Felipe had to climb a steep tall incline to reach their destination. Felipe stayed just a few feet from Selene as they had climbed almost half way to the top: he told her to watch her step when he himself lost his footing on the loose rocks. Felipe fell, head first Selene watched in horror as she was helpless to stop him falling or grab him on the way down. Felipe's head hit a rock on the way down as did his shoulder and leg he finally landed his body twisted at the point where they had began their accent.

Selene called out Felipe however he lay still and did not answer her! Selene's mind flashed back to the day she lost her best friend Amica. She had become friends with Felipe and now another tragedy I'm cursed she thought. I have to do something I cannot let this happen again. Quickly she climbed down the small incline. When Selene reached the body of Felipe she could tell he was still with her however he was badly injured. What can I do? Selene scanned the area around but saw no one in sight.

The Words "If you should ever need me, just think of me" Flooding her mind she remembered the thoughts of the Horse Lord. Instantly Selene closed her eyes and in her mind she screamed "Bodacious Please Help Me I Need You!" Over and Over she repeated these words in her head almost to the point that her head began to hurt. Tears began to well in Selene's eyes as she thought of loosing another friend. She stood there sobbing with her hands over her face helpless!

Selene could not tell how long she had been standing there so she knelt down to check on her new friend he was still with her. Felipe was still unconscious but breathing. She dared not try to move him but she needed to make him comfortable and examine the injuries. As she knelt there some the small pebbles on the ground began to shake. Selene could feel the ground begin to quake under her knees. The longer she knelt by Felipe's side the ground moved underneath her knees. She could hear a great rumbling like she had never heard before. Atop the incline loose rocks and sand began to fall, when she looked up she heard the whinnying of horses it seemed like hundreds of them up there. Just moments afterward Selene saw the Horse Lord running full speed toward her, with his whole heard following after him.

As the Horse Lord slid to a stop he looked at her Selene heard the words what can we do to help you Goddess? Selene said I have to get him help we have to chance moving him I must get him to my Parents. Which of your kind is the fastest? Selene said out loud. The Horse Lord looked at her in disbelief that she had even asked such an absurd question. However he dismissed the question because of the situation. The Horse Lord looked over his shoulder and two large Black horses stood upon each side of him. The Horse Lord walked up beside Felipe and began to bow down then he knelt and lay down. The two black horses walked to Felipe and carefully took the young man's clothes in their mouths and lifted him across the back of their Lord.

The Horse Lord Looked at Selene and though to her climb on and hold him close oh and hold on tight to my mane. The Horse Lord gently rose as not to lose his precious cargo then he bolted forward. The two black horses stayed as close to the Horse Lord as possible. Although it was difficult to run as fast as their Lord they strained to stay one on each side as not to lose Felipe and Selene. As they ran Selene though why did you bring all of your kind? The Horse Lord's thoughts came to her mind I thought you were surrounded by monsters; you screamed so loudly but did not tell me why. I decided I would; need help to defeat them   all.

A quick grin crossed Selene face then she looked back at her friend who lay across the Horse Lord's back limp and still bleeding. Only a little further then mother and father can tend Felipe's wounds, thank you thank you so much you are a wonderful friend Selene though to the Horse Lord. The three horses swept past the river and up the path to the home of Selene. The Horse Lord slowed as to not throw the two off his back. Easily he knelt down to lay on his side again to allow the two black horses to lift Felipe off his back. Selene screamed for her mother and father, already half out the door from the sound. Jalen lifted and carried the young man inside and told Selene to wait outside. Asa followed her mate inside to help him.

Instantly Selene turned to the Horse Lord and threw her arms around his neck sobbing in his long mane. He stood there and let the girl release all the pain she was feeling as he read her thoughts he understood her pain. The Horse Lord thought to her he will be fine you deserve to have another friend besides me to lay your burdens on. Selene rose from his mane and looked at him and thought for a moment another friend I don't even know what you are called. The Horse Lord whinnied something aloud and she heard the words; my name means Magnificent, Bodacious! You can call me Bo! Selene said aloud to Bo "I thank you he would have died if you had not come"! You are welcome she heard in her mind, are you fine now? "Yes" Selene said "but wait please do not go; Felipe and I were on our way to see you he wanted to meet you when I told him how amazing you are". "Really" Bo thought to her. "Yes he says he is fascinated by your kind Selene told him". "Well then I shall wait to meet him! Bo told her in his thoughts. Bo looked too the two black horses and they turned and trotted off in the direction of Bo's herd.

Selene sat on a stump in front to her dwelling as Bo knelt to lie down after the long hard run. As the two rested they waited for some good news about Felipe. However they both wished for the best they both knew that the outcome would be bleak. After an hour or so the two of them began to converse back and forth with their minds. Bo told Selene the story of how he had lost his mate many years ago. Her death was the result of one of mans invasion into the valley where the horse used to dwell. Bo explained how his mate was run until she broke a leg trying to flee mans rope. This is the main reason Bo did not care for humans and why he had moved his kind higher in the landscape.

Selene also shared a story with Bo, she told him of how she and Amica used to sit and watch the horses. How she had dreamed that one day she would ride the back of a horse and command it with only her voice. Furthermore she added that she had told Amica she would one day be a healer of animals. Bo thought to himself I wish Selene had been there when my mate suffered and died, she could have helped to save her life I believed.

Bo had just thought the words the animals are truly blessed that they now have you, when the skin flew open on her dwelling. Jalen emerged and said the young man will be fine; his injuries are not that bad. There is a deep cut to the head and he was knocked unconscious but he is awake now. He has a cut on his leg and his arm is broken but he will heal in a few weeks. The news Jalen had was much better than what Selene expected she was overjoyed when Jalen told her that Felipe asked to see her. She started for the opening then turned to look at Bo who knew that meant to follow her. Selene went inside and Bo stood at the door as he did not fit inside the dwelling.

Selene walked in and said "hello Felipe, I have someone who wants to met you his name is Bo! He carried the two of us home quickly." Felipe looked up and smiled wearily at the both of them and his face lit up when he saw Bo and how truly amazing he really is. Felipe asked Selene to tell Bo thank you and that he thought Bo was a beautiful creature". Selene thought the words in her mind and looked to Bo who nodded his head back to Felipe in return.

Bo thought to Selene I will go now and let the young man rest please tell him we shall see more of each other in a few days time. Selene nodded and in her mind she said I will and thank you for being my friend! Bo nodded again then he backed out of the opening to leave.

Chapter 6
Healing Together

For weeks after the accident Selene and Felipe spent day after day with each other. Jalen had told them it would take six to eight weeks for the arm to heal then he would be completely healed. Selene was grateful that Felipe's injuries were not more severe. As she did not ever wish to lose another friend, she could not go thru that ever again. Felipe secretly loved the company of Selene and he was grateful she had saved his life. He could have died out in the landscape if she had not been there!

The two of them grew closer and closer they made each other laugh and the two of them had so much in common. They both loved and wanted to help the animals. They both knew the landscape around them and they were both the same age! The more they talked they grew closer together and they wanted to spend every second they could together.

Bo as promised visited the two of them often until Felipe was completely healed. The day that Jalen planned to take the splint off Felipe's arm Bo strolled up to Selene's dwelling he was with a young light tan horse the same size as Bo who also had a beautiful long mane and tail. The tan horse was called Rain as it was raining when he was born. Selene, Bo and Rain watched as the splint came off and Felipe began to move and bend his arm. Good as new Jalen told them all. Now you all go have fun and be back in the evening before the meal.

Selene heard the words "how would the two of you like to go for a long ride? Selene looked at Bo and said really and truly you will let me ride you. Bo shook his head and said no in his mind! However this young stallion has told me he wished to be your friend and he agreed to allow you to sit upon him.

Selene thought again you said the two of us? Yes Bo said clearly in her head Felipe shall sit upon my back if you will so tell him. Therefore Selene told Felipe that he could ride upon the back of Bo. Felipe's eyes lit up again and he was overwhelmed with amazement. I can sit upon the most amazing horse in the land? Felipe asked Bo. Bo nodded his head and he bowed down low to the ground for Felipe to get upon his back. Rain did the same he got very low to the ground as Selene was very short so she could get on easily.

The two horses walked side by side until they cleared the rough landscape then two horses looked at each other then suddenly they hopped off their front feet and leaped forward in two steps they were running as fast as they could. Each rider clenched their legs around the horse and held tight with both hands full of the horse's mane. The four of them ran and walked all day Selene interpreted words for Felipe while the horses and she talked with them also they all became as close as a family is together. The four of them had made a complete circle around both villages and back to the river. Bo left Selene, Felipe and Rain all there and said his goodbyes for now and promised to check back often. Rain walked back to Selene's home with the two humans. When they were almost to the dwelling the two stopped and turned to each other and said together I had a wonderful day with you, simultaneously. They both laughed and looked at one another then Felipe reached down to lightly kiss Selene on the lips. Surprised she stood and just stared at him then she reached for Felipe's neck and pulled him closer as she kissed him in return.

"Will you come see me tomorrow I want you to go into the landscape with me to see all my friends and get to know them"? Selene asked looking into Felipe's eyes. He said yes of course I will. The two of them said goodnight Felipe turned and walked toward the village. Rain walked up and nudged Selene she looked at him and said there is a nice place for you to rest around the back of the dwelling if you are tired, you did carry me around all day. Rain nodded as he too walked away to go rest.

Selene however could not rest she was so happy and full of energy as well as filled with something she's not felt before. Now more than before she could not get Felipe out of her mind her thoughts of him his thoughts of her were bouncing around in her head. As Selene bounced into her home her mother asked why so spry. Selene looked at her and said "I am just so happy mother I cannot stand still"! Asa studied her daughters face then she smiled and said "I know what has filled you with joy it is Love"! Love Selene looked at her mother and said "How do you know it is love? I have just had a wonderful day is all"! "I know that look I felt that joy the first time Jalen kissed me"! Asa told her daughter.

Selene's mind started reeling with questions is it really true am I in love, what is it like mother what do I do how do I act around him now all these things she wanted to ask her mother. Asa looked at her and said "just act normal" as if she could read her mind as well". "It will come naturally to the both of you. "I was young once like you"!

The next day soon after the morning meal Selene was dressed and outside speaking with Rain getting to know him better and deciding what they would do this day as Felipe walked up beside Rain and began to stroke him along his mane and body. Good morning to you Selene did you sleep well he asked looking at Selene. Yes I did she replied to him. Then Felipe spoke to Rain and how did you sleep do you like your new home he asked? Rain looked at Selene and told her to tell Felipe he had slept well and he very much liked his new home. Then where are we going today Felipe asked Selene. Just this side of the glades past the Soto village I hear there are animals in need of me there". With the words out of her mouth Rain bowed Low to the ground Selene leaned over his back and Felipe did the same then he rose and turned to walk to their destination. As they walked along Selene told her companions that this would give them a chance to see how a goddess acts and what her purpose is in this land.

Three furlongs before they reached the edge of the glades the three companions noticed several animals and deer running away from the direction they were headed. Rain took it upon himself to seek out the urgency that caused the animals to run. Soon they began to see the dilemma. Three bear cubs rather large in size were raiding nests and destroying burrows as well as being destructive they were playing and breaking branches with nests and even small trees down. Selene said "this is bad I cannot help in this situation Bears are predators I cannot speak with predators". Felipe said "these are not carnivorous bears these eat roots and berries! They are young bears just playing and being naughty" as Felipe began to laugh at the bears playing.

Selene held up her hand as she approached the bears. She thought the words may I please speak with you? The bears stopped and turned toward her. One stood on hind legs he seemed to be the largest of the three. What human we care not to talk to you! The words were garbled in her mind however she could understand the bear. Please I understand you are young and only wish to play and have fun; however you are destroying lives and homes of the other creatures around you! Selene pleaded with the young bears to cease their reckless play and roughhousing. It took several moments and much convincing on Selene's part to get the bear cubs to agree to play somewhere where there was not so much life surrounding them. However the bear cubs agreed to play next to a small clearing nearer the glades. Of course the bear cubs decided it was best closer to the glades as they loved to roll in the mud and water there anyway!

Selene then spoke to all the animals in the area and helped as many as she could to rebuild or relocate the homes that had been destroyed. Felipe and Rain also did what they could to help and were exhausted at the end of the day. The cubs had been playing in the area for weeks and destroyed much in their playtime each day they had visited. With all the creatures satisfied that she Felipe and Rain had done all possible to help the animals thanked the three for their help and all retreated to their new and rebuilt homes for the evening!

Selene Felipe and Rain all started toward their homes as well. When the three reached the Ritke village Selene and Felipe said their goodnights with a touch followed by a long gentle kiss. Selene climbed back atop Rain and they turned toward home. On the way to her home Selene had thoughts of always being with Felipe. She thought how wonderful it would be to have him as her life mate for the rest of her life. Selene hated it when she had to leave him or when she saw him have to walk away from her to go to his home. She never wanted to have to leave him again she though only of him and what a life with him would be like.

Chapter 7
Be Mine Selene

Many months had passed since Selene had met Felipe their bond grew stronger each day they spent together. Selene's powers as The Moon Goddess grew stronger as well she was secure in who she was and what her purpose was in the landscape. Rain stayed close to Selene as their bond grew greater as well. Rain accepted Felipe as a friend and the three of them were inseparable.

Selene and Rain took the day off from traveling around the landscape seeking out animals in need of help as recently all seemed to be a peace and well being she wasn't needed as frequently. The two sat and talked within their minds Rain turned his head to see Felipe approaching. Rain bowed his head in greeting Felipe did the same? Selene said hello to Felipe, and he replied back the same to her. Felipe looked at Rain and spoke "please take the day off and allow Selene and I to walk together we have matters to discuss". Rain looked at Selene and she nodded her approval to the request as did Rain.

As they walked along Felipe began to speak to Selene saying he loved being with her and just being in her presents then he asked her "can a Goddess be one's life mate". Selene stopped suddenly and looked into Felipe's eyes "why are you asking this of me". "Because I Love You Selene I want you to be mine" Felipe told her. Felipe turned to Selene looked her in the eyes and said will you please be my life mate! "I Love You".

You wish me to be your life mate Selene jumped at Felipe and hung from his neck tears fell as she uttered the word "yes Felipe my love I will be your life mate"! Felipe picked her up then walked over and sat on a Hugh rock with her in his lap holding her. Both so in love, both so happy, both so young and full of life and hope they held each other the rest of the day not speaking words only being with each other. Selene though this would be the best day of her life.

The two sat and time slipped by so quickly they didn't realize they had not eaten as the day grew dark Felipe said "I will walk you home there is much to do". Selene nodded and they walked back to her dwelling they said their goodnights and kissed as he turned to go back to the village.

On the way back however they had agreed to talk to her father and mother the very next day for a blessing. A young man had to lay prone before the parents of the girl that he wished to be his life mate. Furthermore he had to pass any test that the father requested of him in order to show his ability to protect as well as provide for his intended life mate. If he could not do this he was not deemed worthy to have a girl in the village.

The very next morning Jalen pulled back the skin to exit his dwelling he saw Felipe lying in front of his eyes. Felipe was lying on the ground before him. Jalen smiled as he spoke to Felipe. What is your intention Felipe? Felipe spoke "I come to ask you to test me and find me worthy of your blessing to take Selene as my life mate". "I pray that you not be lenient upon me test me harshly please".

Jalen spoke to Felipe and said " rise, give me two days to confer with Asa we shall decide upon a just test for you" You may not see Selene for the two days until you return in the same manner as you did today". Felipe nodded in agreement as he turned to leave.

Jalen went about his day making visits in the village checking on the members. Asa went about her gathering the roots and herbs needed for medicines. However she was not aware of the request Felipe had made of Jalen. Jalen returned home later that evening then Jalen explained the situating to her. "Do you agree to allow me to test Felipe worthy of taking Selene as his life mate"? Jalen asked Asa as she looked not too surprised to hear this news. Asa thought only for a few seconds and said "I do agree to allow you to test Felipe"!

"What test shall we give Felipe to prove him worthy" Asa asked Jalen. Jalen spoke and added that Felipe had requested they not be easy on him while testing him. Jalen told Asa they had two days before he would return furthermore he has requested that he not see Selene for the two days. Jalen decided that the request alone would be difficult for Felipe as the two of them were inseparable! Asa asked how Felipe had reacted to Jalen's demand and he told her he agreed if he disapproved it did not show! Both decided to tell Selene before she became angered at Felipe for not coming around for the two days. Therefore they found her and explained that there would be times when the two would need to be apart and this was only a small portion of Felipe's testing.

The next morning Asa and Jalen devised two tests that they deemed worthy of their daughters mate. The first would be the life of the great black cat that had tried to attack Selene, if the cat had tried to attack Selene that meant he would attack other humans and was a danger to the tribe. Felipe would bring the head and pelt; the head of the great cat for the tribe and the pelt to Selene. The second test would be a three day quest to retrieve greatly needed Persimmon Fruit far away from the safety of the village and its members. The tests should only take one week at the most. However that is only if the great cat is easy to find and if Felipe passed each test then the two could become as one.

The Ritke would hold a massive celebration a feast then the leader would stand with the father and mother of the village girl and give their public blessing upon the union of the two. Furthermore everyone would pray for the two to have many children as children are the future of the tribe and the Ritke way of life.

Jalen, Asa as well as Selene went on about their lives and their daily chores for the next two days. On the morning of the third day as Jalen and Asa walked out of their dwelling Felipe was lying face down at the front of their feet.

Jalen requested Felipe to stand and hear the tests that were required of him. Felipe was to hunt down the Great Black Cat that had attacked Selene. Felipe was to present head to the leader of the tribe and the pelt to his future life mate. Next Felipe would travel several days to retrieve the fruit or Persimmon berries an important fruit to the village this is used as a vitamin supplement as well as to cure many illnesses. The older tribe members use this fruit to determine future events.

Therefore Felipe was instructed to go and pack for his tests and return when the both were completed. Felipe could complete the test in the order that he saw fit as long as the requirements were met. The order was his to decide therefore he decided to do them both at the same time he would search for the cat while on his way to retrieve the wild persimmons!

Felipe asked permission to see Selene before he was to leave and Jalen granted his request. Felipe and Selene said their goodbyes then Selene told him to be strong and return to her as soon as he safely could. Felipe went on his way to prepare for the tests set before him. If Felipe was scared he did not let Selene see his fear. Each young man in the village had to prove he was an expert hunter therefore this test was hard as well as dangerous. Felipe truly wanted to be the one to bring in the head of the cat. The great cat lurked too close to the villages seeking easy, weak, small prey. The great cat was feared by all the villagers as they had to watch their children and food stores closely.

Felipe devised a good strategy for killing the great cat once he came upon his tracks. He had been on several hunts with the man that took him from the Soto village after his parents had died. Therefore he knew he had to stay downwind of the cat as well as he had to be as quiet as a tiny mouse on his feet. One mistake one miss, with his spear or arrow it would cost him his life.

It would be slightly out of his way to get the Persimmons but he would venture into the great cats territory on the way and claim the cat first. The cat was brave and smart therefore Felipe had to outsmart his quarry to fulfill his test to be worthy of Jalen and Asa's blessing to have Selene. I must succeed I will succeed. Selene and I will be together I am worthy of her and her love Felipe thought to himself as he walked to his home. Once he reached his home he told the man who had taken him in that he had asked Jalen to test him worthy of Selene to be his life mate. Furthermore he said what the test entailed and that he was not afraid to fulfill either of them. Felipe said I wanted you to know so you will be proud of me you have raised me well and taught me to be an excellent hunter. I thank you I shall return to the village and Selene soon.

Chapter 8

My Tests My Quest

Felipe took a large skin bag from a shelf he packed some fruits, bread, and a few other much needed supplies. Felipe did not know how long his journey would be therefore he also carried a sharp long knife and extra arrows for his bow strapped to the bag. A heavy spear stood against the wall as he took the spear in his hand he thought to himself. This is my test my quest for the one I love to see I am worthy of her. I will kill the Great Black Cat with this spear. With that thought he threw back the skin to his dwelling and bolted out the opening on his quest.

Felipe had to journey thru the Great Cats territory to reach the land where the persimmons grew in abundance. He hoped he would get lucky and find the cats tracks on the way. Little did he know the cat would find him?

Felipe walked along as he thought, should I go by and see Selene before I set off on my test? No he thought he had said his goodbyes earlier and he did not wish to worry Selene as he had assured her that he would be fine and would return to her safely.

Therefore Felipe continued on his way he must focus now he could not think of anything except his test that was ahead of him. If he did lose his concentration even for a second it could mean his life then Selene would have nothing but a broken heart as well as a lie if he did not return to her as promised.

Felipe cleared his mind and thought only of the Panther the great cat that almost took Selene's life had Bo not intervened. He had several more furlongs to travel before he was even close to the cats' territory. Never the less his mind began to full with strategies and tactics on ways to outwit the great cat. The panther had not lived this long by being careless. Felipe would need all of his hunting skills to find and overpower a predator of this magnitude!

Felipe walked and walked keeping his mind on his target when he neared the area where Selene had told him the cat had attacked her and could have taken her life. He pursued any sign that the cat was close. The normal signs like footprints, fur on tree branches or underbrush, signs of a fresh kill left in a tree or buried to be finished off later. Felipe did see old footprints and hoof prints so this must have been where Bo fought the cat off. The further into the cats' territory Felipe stayed tense, alert he used every sense he had, sharp eyes, keen hearing, intense sense of smell. However he heard smelled or saw nothing. Felipe finally decided to wait and see if the Panther would return to his hunting grounds. Therefore he found a spot with thick brush behind him. This way he could see what if anything was coming at him from the front. Felipe would be trapped but this was a tactical advantage. Furthermore the cat would be tempted because of the fact Felipe would be trapped. Felipe laid out his weapons and waited for the darkness to come.

As Felipe sat and patiently waited he took handfuls of grass leaves and dirt he rubbed them on his body and covered his weapons with the grass. This would keep the human smell down and or mask it from the great cat. Panthers have a keen unique sense of smell. If he could leave just a hint of his scent the cat would search for him. However if he were still in the night he would have the element of surprise.

Now he was ready for the cat he sat rock solid and waited the only thing he let move on his body were his eyes as he scanned the landscape. Hours passed as each time he heard the slightest sound his eyes quickly searched for the cause of the sound. The hours passed and even though he heard many noises he did not hear anything big enough to make the sound of the cat he hunted.

Felipe sat the entire night without gaining the results he wanted he saw no great cat not even a hint of the cat anywhere. Therefore he determined that the cat must have been hunting that night in another area of his territory. With the dawn Felipe decided he should rest before continuing on his quest to find the Persimmons' and so he lay down to rest for a few hours.

When Felipe awoke much to his surprise he felt a tickling on his nose he jumped back opened his eyes to see a plump white rabbit sitting before his face. Once he was fully awake he determined that this must be the same white rabbit Selene has seen when she visited this area. Felipe wondered how the rabbit had survived being this plump he was a tasty meal for any predator out here in the landscape.

Obviously this little creature needed a safe and secure home Felipe decided to take the rabbit with him as he scooped the large bundle of fur up and put him in his large bag he carried on his back the rabbit sat still and quietly as to agree he wanted to go with Felipe. The rabbit would need a name so Felipe decided to call the plump white rabbit Chaucer. As he walked along he wondered how the little rabbit had come to be alone furthermore he agreed with Selene when she said the rabbit had once been a pet of someone. Apparently they had taken great care of the rabbit and he would try to do the same.

Felipe's greatest concern was to protect Chaucer from the great cat as the rabbit would make an excellent meal he would have to leave the rabbit in a safe place out of the way while he hunted the cat again. Felipe's mind now turned to the Persimmon fruit; he needed gather as many as he could to return them to his village for the much needed medicine. The area the Persimmons grew was still many furlongs away so Felipe talked to Chaucer to pass the time while he walked along. Felipe now wished that he had stopped back by to see Selene and have her to ask Rain to carry him on this long journey. However that might have shown Jalen that he was lazy and unwilling to make the quest on his own and that was the last thing he wished to appear as.

Felipe walked long into the evening and grew weary therefore he decided he would rest for the night he found a nice spot to let Chaucer out of the bag. The place he chose was close to a small trickle of water and the ground was grassy and soft. The both settled in for the nights rest. Chaucer snuggled close to Felipe for warmth and security then faded off to sleep.

The next morning Chaucer was a few feet away nibbling on the foliage and hopping around. Felipe woke up and looked around for something to add to his own food supply. He found some yummy berries and some bananas then put them into his large skin bag of supplies. Once he was satisfied that Chaucer was full he again scooped the rabbit up and continued on his quest to find the Persimmon fruit.

Growing closer to the area where the Persimmons' grow Felipe talked to Chaucer as he walked to pass the time. Felipe rather enjoyed the company of the plump little rabbit. Chaucer sat quietly while he rode in the large skin bag on Felipe's back. Felipe finally reached the area where the persimmon fruit grew in abundance. However his large bag was not large enough for the amount of the fruit he needed to take back to the village. Therefore Felipe needed to fashion some way to carry a great supply of the fruit back with him. He looked around for some time but without success. Therefore he decided he would have to weave a basket from the vines hanging from the trees. Even though this would be time consuming he had to take the time in order to complete his test.

Felipe took out his knife as he carefully sat down the bag that Chaucer was riding in. he began to pull down strong long vines and lay them aside so he could weave them into a basket. It took Felipe the better part of the day to craft a basket large enough to hold about three bushels of the fruit. Felipe figured this should be sufficient to use to make the medicine for the tribe. Furthermore any remaining fruit could be dried and also used as medicine if it were needed. Once the basket was finished before Felipe began to gather the fruit he decided he needed to eat something to keep his strength up. So Felipe found a shaded place and took a few moments to eat some of the food he had brought with him then he picked one of the dark red-orange colored persimmons and ate it as well. Persimmons are packed with vitamins and this would help him complete his test he had to remain strong for the long journey back furthermore he still had to hunt the great cat.

Once his meal was finished Felipe began to gather the greener Persimmons to take with him as he did not want them to spoil on the journey back to the village. However once he had gathered all the fruits that he wanted the basket was difficult to carry. Again Felipe looked for a solution to the problem. He decided the best way to carry the fruits back was to fashion a travois' to the basket. Using two long poles and some more vine he tied the basket between the two poles this way he dragged the poles and the basket. This took a great deal of weight off of his back and shoulders leaving his arms to carry most of the burden. Once the fruit was secure Felipe placed Chaucer in the bag put the bag on his back and picked up the ends of the travois and began to drag it behind him back toward the great cats' territory.

The journey back went much slower than the trip to reach the fruited area. Felipe pulled and walked pulled and walked each step grew harder and harder. It would have been worse had he not had the travois but it was still difficult. He would not falter he could not fail he had to keep going and finish his quest. The hardest part was still to come therefore he could not begin to tire now with only this little a load he was strong and determined to fulfill his test. So Felipe continued on putting one foot in front of the other pulling with all his might. It had taken time to fashion the basket and make the travois then gather fruit so his light began to fade from that day and he grew weary from the burden. Therefore Felipe decided he should rest. He needed to let Chaucer eat and drink and he needed to eat and rest as well. Felipe took Chaucer out and sat him down so he could eat and drink. Felipe ate another Persimmon this again would help him regain his strength and complete the task ahead. Then the both again settled in for the night or rest to continue on the next day.

Chapter 9

It's Hunting Me

The next morning brought the warm light of the sun to Felipe's face as he opened his eyes again he saw the plump white rabbit sitting before his face waiting for him to wake up. Felipe sat up and took Chaucer in his arms the fur was silky soft and the rabbit was warm and soothing to the touch. They both sat in each other's company for a while then Felipe told Chaucer they should be on their way they had another long day ahead. Felipe put Chaucer down and he hopped over to his large skin bag and waited to be put inside. Felipe picked him up and gently put him inside the bag and placed the bag on his back. Then again he reached for the poles to continue on his way back to the Ritke village and beloved Selene.

As Felipe walked and pulled the travois it made a scraping sound the sound was quite loud so it was difficult to hear or concentrate on anything but the noise. However after several hours of walking and pulling Chaucer began to wiggle around inside the bag. Felipe decided the rabbit needed to stretch out or maybe relieve itself therefore he stopped and let Chaucer out to do what he needed to while he ate something and got him a drink. Felipe put the bag down and opened it to let Chaucer out but the rabbit came out reluctantly. Chaucer only went a few feet away from Felipe then quickly returned to his friend. Felipe sat and ate his meal and rested a bit then the two resumed their journey on toward the great cats' territory.

Felipe walked and pulled as he listened to the dragging scraping sound he found it annoying. Never the less it was something he would just have to deal with until he reached his destination. Felipe determined it would take him a day and most of the next to reach the area where the great cat lived and hunted. Then Felipe would have to find a safe place for Chaucer and his precious cargo he had been towing back. Then he could take the time necessary to find and kill this man killing cat. Felipe walked and pulled the travois the rest of the day to the point of exhaustion then into the dark he found a spot and rested as he had the nights before. So Felipe and Chaucer could continue on their way back to complete his test.

However when Felipe let Chaucer out of the skin bag again he was reluctant to venture off as he usually did. Felipe just passed it off as the little rabbit had already become very attached to him. Felipe did not realize that he should have headed the little rabbits being cautious. Felipe was so tired from walking and pulling on the heavy load all day all he wanted to do was rest. So Felipe gave Chaucer a small amount of water for the night then fell off to sleep once he lay down.

His eyes again opened to the plump rabbit in his face awaiting Felipe to get up and face the day. Again they ate drank and fueled up for the long hard day of work that would bring them closer to the end of their journey. Therefore once Chaucer was tucked safely away in his bag Felipe picked up the poles once again and headed for the area where the deadly cat lived. Several hours had gone by and again Chaucer began to wiggle in the bag except this time the wiggle seemed much more urgent. Felipe stopped to put down the poles to the basket as he reached around for his bag that carried Chaucer a cold chill ran up the back of his neck he heard the big cat's heavy breathing.

Felipe did not turn around he could tell the Panther was close in fact right behind him. His spear was atop the basket tied to it securely. His bow and arrows were attached to the bag on his back all Felipe had was his medium size hunting knife. Slowly he moved his right hand toward the knife while he thought he is hunting me. How stupid of me to let down my guard I could not hear around me for the scraping sounds the basket made and I let him walk right up behind me. Before the next thought could enter his mind it was too late the great cat leaped and hit Felipe astride his back. Felipe did manage to unsheathe the knife and hold on to it because his life literally did depend upon it. The cat sunk his long teeth into Felipe's arm the pain was almost more than he could bear the cats jaws were strong enough to crush a man's skull.

With his knife in his right hand the cat had hold of Felipe reached around with his left hand and grabbed a massive handful of the cat's fur. He pulled with all the strength he had to pull away from the cat. He had to be facing the cat as the cat now had the advantage over him. He managed to pull around somewhat facing the panther ripping his own flesh while doing so the pain tore thru his arm.

However he still grasp the knife, he took the knife in his left hand and stabbed the cat in the ribs. The cat let go of the hold on Felipe's arm. The cat took a small step back and slashed across Felipe's chest, Felipe screamed in agony.

Not thinking Felipe reacted and lunged at the cat slashing with the knife. Again Felipe stabbed the powerful cat; the cat shook its head and turned to lunge for Felipe's throat with both hands free now Felipe put the knife back in the right hand and reached out to meet the cat mid lunge. The knife hit its mark the cat's heart just behind the ribs on its left side. The massive cat landed atop Felipe he could barely move under the cat's weight the great cats flinched several times still fighting for breath and holding onto life. It was a lost cause Felipe had wounded the cat's most vital organs its lungs and its heart. The great cat was finally dead. Felipe had actually killed the great cat with his hands and a simple knife. He struggled to get out from under the weight of the dead animal. It was difficult as Felipe was injured this was not the outcome he had hoped for. Never the less the result was the one he wanted he was alive and the man hunter was dead.

Felipe managed to slide a few feet away from the cat's body and get his bag off his back. He checked to see if Chaucer was ok the little rabbit shook with fear and Felipe lifted Chaucer with his good arm to reassure the little rabbit he was again safe. It took some time before Felipe and the rabbit both could take a deep steady breath. Felipe told Chaucer "I think he was trying to eat you not me little one." Then he thought softly we got him and no need to worry over him ever again.

Felipe took some nearby leaves and some plants he rolled the plants between his hands and placed the leaves on the place the cat bit his arm then put a larger leaf on that then tied it with a small leather strap. Felipe's arm began to feel better once he felt the numbing effect of the leaves. However the large gashes across his chest bled profusely he had to stop the bleeding quickly or he would not be able to continue. Felipe found some moss and filled the claw marks with the moss then he pressed his shirt down and held the pressure on it for a while. His chest began to feel better and the bleeding did finally stop.

Felipe removed the blood soaked moss and replaced it with fresh he then tied his shirt tight around his chest to keep it from bleeding again. Now he had to push thru the pain and finish his test. He had to remove the head and skin the panther. Felipe put the head of the panther at the bottom on the travois while he removed the shiny black pelt of the cat. Then he wrapped the head inside the skin and tied these to the travois as well. Felipe felt as he was moving in slow motion as his body hurt. The cats mouth and claws are filled with germs and bacteria that can make a man deathly ill. If Felipe could not get to Jalen in time to be treated he feared the worse.

Felipe walked to the front of the travois picked up the poles and began to pull and walk only now he was headed for home. This day was going fast therefore that meant he had to walk long into the night he was at least two days maybe more away for home. Felipe's thoughts turned to the cat again how did he let the cat run upon him like that. He knew in the back of his mind that cats travel many furlongs while hunting and looking for a mate. Felipe was lucky that he was only injured and he had not lost his life to a predator like that. He had saved the village from the cat now he had to think about the injuries the cat had caused he was still in danger.

Felipe walked as fast as he could and pulled as hard as he could he had to make it back to the village with the fruit and the remains of the cat. He had to walk into the village on his own strength and present the tribes oldest member or the chef of the tribe. Then he had to reach Jalen to give him the fruit then he had to give the pelt to Selene.

The light began to fade around Felipe however he continued to walk and pull. Felipe continued to drive himself, I have to pull I have to keep walking, I cannot stop. He kept repeating this over and over again to himself pushing and driving himself not to quit. Felipe was so tired, sore and he began to feel somewhat ill. The travois seemed much heavier with every step but Felipe continued for a few more hours until finally he had to rest. Felipe put down the poles and he sat down to eat and to drink something. First he reached for a Persimmon this would help his immune system and his strength while he slept. He let Chaucer out of the bag so he could eat and drink also.

It felt good to rest; it was helpful that he had the Persimmons. Without them he might not make it home but it would be better to have the knowledge that Jalen did. He could make something to use to ward off the infection that began to set into his body from the bite and the scratches.

Felipe finished his meal he tucked Chaucer under his arm and held the little rabbit close for warmth as he fell asleep from exhaustion. Chaucer stayed tucked in close to Felipe while he did his best to look after Felipe. A rabbit may be small and seem helpless however he could wake Felipe if he were to hear something or smell danger.

Chaucer let Felipe sleep until the sun began to rise. Then the little rabbit got up in Felipe's face nose to nose and he nudged Felipe's face. Felipe did not move he continued to sleep. Chaucer could sense the need for Felipe to get up on his feet. Chaucer had to wake Felipe up at all costs. So Chaucer put his front paws on Felipe's face and rocked back and forward trying to wake Felipe. This seemed to work Felipe began to move and arouse. Felipe awoke to a face full of white soft fur. As he spoke softly to Chaucer he said "I am still here with you little one, not to worry".

Felipe sat up and reached for Chaucer to put him in the bag but the rabbit hopped away from his reach. This puzzled Felipe however he reached for the rabbit once more. Chaucer again hopped away; Felipe decided that this meant Chaucer would rather walk instead of ride inside the bag. Therefore he swung the bag across his back and reached to pick up the poles to the travois. Once again he and the little rabbit headed in the direction of home medicine and his love Selene. He could make it only one more day and he should be home he could make it he was rested. He did not feel well the infection was beginning to travel thru his body. Felipe ignored the sick feeling and thought of home his love and the life they would live with each other.

Long into the heat of the day Felipe struggled to pull the load and find the strength to continue. Felipe managed to pull and pull with all the might in his body. Finally he told Chaucer he had to rest for a bit and drink then they could continue on their way. Chaucer stopped and sat waiting for a drink of cool water from the skin Felipe carried. They both drank and refreshed their bodies. The humidity in the rain forest was stifling. Felipe could feel the sickness more and more he grew weaker and his vision began to blur.

The longer he sat the weaker he felt, Felipe slowly managed to get to his feet. As he reached for the poles to resume his journey he slightly stumbled. Finally he regained his balance and picked up the travois and began to pull. Chaucer hopped on a little way ahead to see exactly where they were from home. Chaucer realized that he and Felipe were close to the river he knew this river it smelled like the girl he had met in the landscape they called her goddess. The scent was weak and old but yes she had traveled this way often. In fact the goddess had been this way a few days before.

Chaucer stayed close to Felipe several hours passed as Felipe pulled his load growing weaker and weaker. It was hard to pull the heavy load thru the thick brush close to the river but he had to go on he was so close to home now. The more he struggled the heavy load grew harder to pull. Felipe could not see his vision blurred again and he fell forward.

Chapter 10
Please Help Man

Chaucer stopped turned and went back to where Felipe lie still in the grass. Chaucer touched Felipe's face with his nose Felipe felt hot. The little rabbit wasted no time he jumped over Felipe's body and began to run in the direction of the scent of the goddess. The light faded in the sky this was a dangerous time to be a small rabbit.

Predators come out at night to feed. Chaucer ran along a small path by the river another rabbit used this path. It was tiny that rabbit must have been much smaller than Chaucer. But this path led to an opening where the Goddess's scent was much stronger. She was not there so he followed the scent again he had to find her. Chaucer ran and ran until finally he was at the home of Selene the one they call the Moon Goddess.

Chaucer went up to the skin sniffed again yes this is it she is here. He hopped inside it was dark only a fire burned it took a moment for his small round eyes to see where he was going. He did not see Selene. He did see a body a warm body breathing the little rabbit jumped up onto the person laying there sleeping.

Jalen bolted up and awake when Chaucer landed on him. "What Is This, What is Going On He yelled" of course this woke Asa and Selene as well. Once Selene was awake she heard the rabbit's thoughts, Help, man sick, need Goddess, please, medicine, big cat got him, help, come, follow me! The rabbit's thoughts were garbled. Selene quickly told her father its Felipe he needs medicine the panther attacked him and the little rabbit come quickly follow him father please hurry!

The darkness was unkind they could barely see Chaucer he ran as fast as he possibly could go. His friend had saved him from the big cat he had to help him. Selene and Jalen fought to keep up with the plump little rabbit. For such a fat one he ran quite quickly. It took them about an hour to reach the place where Felipe had collapsed. Chaucer was there beside Felipe with his paws upon his face to comfort him. Felipe opened his eyes to Chaucer and said "hey little one just a little longer we will be home".

Jalen arrived he rolled Felipe over to assess the damage to find the cause of him laying there. Jalen saw the make shift bandages on Felipe's' arm and felt the moss across his chest. The cat must have bit him and clawed him across the chest. We have to get him home Selene quickly. Selene closed her eyes though inside her head Rain I Need You Please Come Quickly follow my Voice to the River. Again she had to depend upon her fast and surefooted friend. They waited patiently with Felipe for Rain to come.

For Rain the trip was only a few short moments of running to find Selene once he arrived she thought. Can you please carry Felipe and father home he needs medicine there to heal? Rain bowed his head and his body Jalen and Selene laid Felipe across the back of the big stout horse and Rain stood up and bolted for home. She heard I will be back for you as well as Rain was leaving.

Selene bent down and took the little rabbit into her arms. Now I must thank you for what you have done my little furry friend. Thank you for helping the man I love. He might have died. Then Selene heard man, saved me, cat eat me, man hurt, help, man, please! The Cat was after you Felipe did not hunt the cat? Selene wondered if this would count in the test. Felipe had to hunt and kill the cat not just stop it from killing another animal. Selene quickly put the thought out of her head.

She looked and found the travois that Felipe refused to leave. Everything he was required to bring back was atop the travois. The Panthers head, its skin. Even a large hand woven basket full of the persimmons the medicinal fruit needed for both tribes. Felipe did what was required of him however he did not return on his own. Would this effect the decision Jalen would make about his worthiness'.

Furthermore should she leave the travois out here or should she ask Rain to help her get it to her home. After all that was Felipe's destination as he was so close to her home. No Selene decided she would finish taking the travois to her home for Felipe.

Rain returned with the news that Jalen was attending Felipe's needs so she knew her lover was in the best place he could be. Rain, will you again help me carry this back to my home? It is a travois a man can drag it or it can be laid across a horse's back and pulled to make the load easier. Rain agreed to help again. Selene used straps of skins in Felipe's' bag to affix the travois comfortably to Rain's back she walked alongside the massive horse. She thanked Rain again for his help to her and Felipe.

Once they arrived back home Selene removed the travois from Rain then she hurried inside to see how Felipe was doing. Jalen quickly told her that Felipe would be fine the infection had not spread to any vital organs. Furthermore that Jalen had given him the medicine to fight off the infection and it would only be a few days and he would be right and strong once again.

When he regains his strength and his wits we will find out how he came to be in the landscape collapsed. Selene asked her father what of the tests he did not fully complete his test. However he did have everything with him that he was supposed to bring back to us. All that you and mother set upon him he fulfilled. Felipe almost died trying to finish his test for me. Jalen told her he would consult with the Father of the tribe the oldest member or the chef. Furthermore he would take Asa as a witness for Felipe to ask the outcome of the decision. Some exceptions could be made in certain situations. Maybe this would be one of those exceptions. If not then Felipe would have to be retested with a new set of requests. Once Felipe regains his strength we shall all go before the tribe and take the head of the man killer. I'm sure the old one will see that Felipe is worthy of you as his life mate.

The next day Felipe awoke weak and still very ill however he asked Jalen "where is the little white rabbit is it ok"? Jalen answered oh yes the rabbit is fine in fact it only leaves your bedside to go out for necessities then she returns to your side. Felipe looked down and saw that Chaucer lay in a bed of straw that Selene had gathered for her nest. It turns out that the rabbit was plump with ten baby rabbit's. All now there for Felipe to care for once he regained his health. Apparently all the stresses of the last few days threw her into delivery. She saved your life friend Jalen told Felipe. Felipe said well I guess we will have to change your name little one. The rabbit looked and shook her head in a no fashion. Ok Chaucer it is and it shall be. Felipe tried to laugh but it still hurt badly to even move.

When Felipe was stronger Jalen and Asa explained the details to him of the test and that it not being finished; he may be retested. The decision lay with the oldest member of the tribe or the chef. In two more days Felipe was much better not fully back to full strength but he was well enough to meet the tribe elder. Felipe stood in the center of Jalen Asa Selene and the oldest member of the tribe. Jalen explained the test's he had set for Felipe as well as the accomplishments Felipe had made. Furthermore he explained that Felipe was attacked from behind by the great Panther. Therefore could not finish the test completely because of his injuries and infection from said injuries.

The elder listened then he sat quietly for a moment then spoke to Felipe and said "bring forth the head of this great cat" So Felipe presented the head to the elder. The blood of Felipe was still on the cat's mouth! This was evidence of the events presented. The elder again spoke and said "you did complete your test and you did kill this man killer" therefore I grant you the life and find you worthy of the one the animals call Moon Goddess as your life mate. Jalen must also agree to this decision or he can grant you one more test to see you worthy of his daughter". Everyone turned to Jalen to see what he would say over the matter. Jalen stood again and said "I do agree with the elder he is truly worthy of my daughter no more test are required". Selene ran to the side of Felipe and clenched his hand within hers.

Asa stood and said "they will be joined in eight days time for life". There were preparations' to be made Selene and Felipe both had to be cleansed and blessed by their families. Selene and Felipe kissed and held each other in love as they said their goodbyes for the seven days that followed they could not see each other while cleansing.

The Ritke believed that before a couple could be joined they must be clean inside as well as out. The men and women could only eat certain foods during this period. Nuts, berries, fresh fruit, fresh vegetables, no meats of any kind. Only these things can be eaten for the seven days. The body must be cleaned in the river for one hour twice a day for the seven days.

Then on the day of the joining both Felipe and Selene will be blessed by their parents and the elder. Since Felipe has no parents only his guardian the guardian must bless Felipe before they can be joined. After the joining there will be a great feast with dancing and blessings from the tribe.

Chapter 11
Bless Us

The seven days had passed all the preparations' had been made. This was the day of the joining of Selene and Felipe. This was also the day they and the union were to be blessed by the entire tribe beginning with their families.

Selene sat inside her home awaiting the time to get ready to spend the rest of her life with Felipe; Asa came in carrying a white dress made of snow rabbit fur. This was the softest, whitest fur from the purest rabbit. These furs were traded for several years ago when Asa's mother made her joining dress. Selene held the dress before her and tears began to well in her and her mother's eyes. Then Asa helped Selene put the dress on. Asa then braided Selene's long beautiful dark black hair and tied it with woven white horse hairs. A necklace of Pearls and feathers was laced around Selene's young slender neckline. Jalen walked in looked at a woman were his baby girl used to be. It is time to go to the clearing. So the family walked together Asa now carried Sticky in the bag. Rain followed behind them.

Selene wondered if Bo the horse lord would come to see the joining. However as they grew closer she saw a ring of horses all around the clearing. Bo Stood beside Felipe at the mouth of the clearing. As Selene approached all the horses Bowed down low Selene could hear all the blessings from each of them. The last one she heard was from Bo may you and Felipe has a blessed life with many young in your future. Selene looked at Bo and Bowed low to the ground to give him the respect he greatly deserved. It was an exception that horses were allowed to be present at a joining. However this was no ordinary joining. This was a brave man joining a Goddess.

Felipe looked at Selene and soaked in her beauty with his eyes. He thought to himself he was the most blessed man in the tribe that Selene had accepted his request to be his life mate. Felipe and Selene each stood beside one another as the elder of the tribe asked who would be the first to bless this joining. A few feet behind Felipe a man's voice said "I shall be the first to bless Felipe. Felipe's guardian spoke Felipe has grown with me from a small child I knew his parents they would be proud. Felipe has become strong and wise in his few years he has made a wise choice I bless him and the one they call The Moon Goddess".

Jalen then spoke up I will speak next. I bless this joining of my daughter Selene and the man brave enough to ask to make her his life mate. This will be a great union and they will be the future of this people. Asa then spoke I too wish to bless the joining of Felipe and Selene this man is brave and has a pure heart he will be true to her and to our life here.

Finally the elder spoke up he said I have watched the two grow in this tribe. Selene has done many great things with the gifts the gods in heaven have given to her. I bless this joining of her and Felipe she shall teach him to speak to the animals as well as their children so our people will be in peace. "Is there another blessing from one here" the elder asked? No one else came forth but Selene I have a blessing from the Horse lord named bodacious his name means Magnificent. Selene introduced Bo to the Village. She spoke for him "I am grateful to our Goddess for bringing understanding to my kind and the great gifts she gave my kind. Now the man and the horse can be helpers to one another. I bless this mating of the two my friend Felipe and the Goddess".

Bo turned and walked away a few steps raised his head high then he and all horses there bowed low to the two of them. The tribe then all stood at once and said we all bless this joining. The elder turned and looked at the two and said "be joined, be happy, be fertile, and be strong. Now be one".

The horses stomped their feet and neighed loud the villagers yelled cheered and drums sounded. Felipe took Selene into his arms kissed her and held her tight. The sound was defining as the two held each other the ground shook under their feet. This union would truly be truly blessed and favored by god.

Long into the night the celebration went on. Felipe's' guardian walked up to the two of them and told Felipe something in his ear. Felipe thanked the man and then he looked at Selene. Felipe took Selene's hand and quickly led her away from the crowd and commotion. Just outside the crowd Rain stood off to himself. Felipe walked up to Rain and whispered something into his ear. Rain Bowed down Felipe put Selene upon Rain's back then he also climbed atop the strong horse's back. Rain took off toward the river behind the village. There all off to itself stood a two room shelter. Felipe's guardian started building this as a new home for the two. Felipe and Selene would have to finish the dwelling the way they wanted it. There was even a nice soft dirt spot for Rain beside the shelter for a horse.

Felipe hopped down off Rain took Selene in his arms and carried her into the dwelling to begin their new life and long love together.

Made in the USA
Monee, IL
17 April 2023